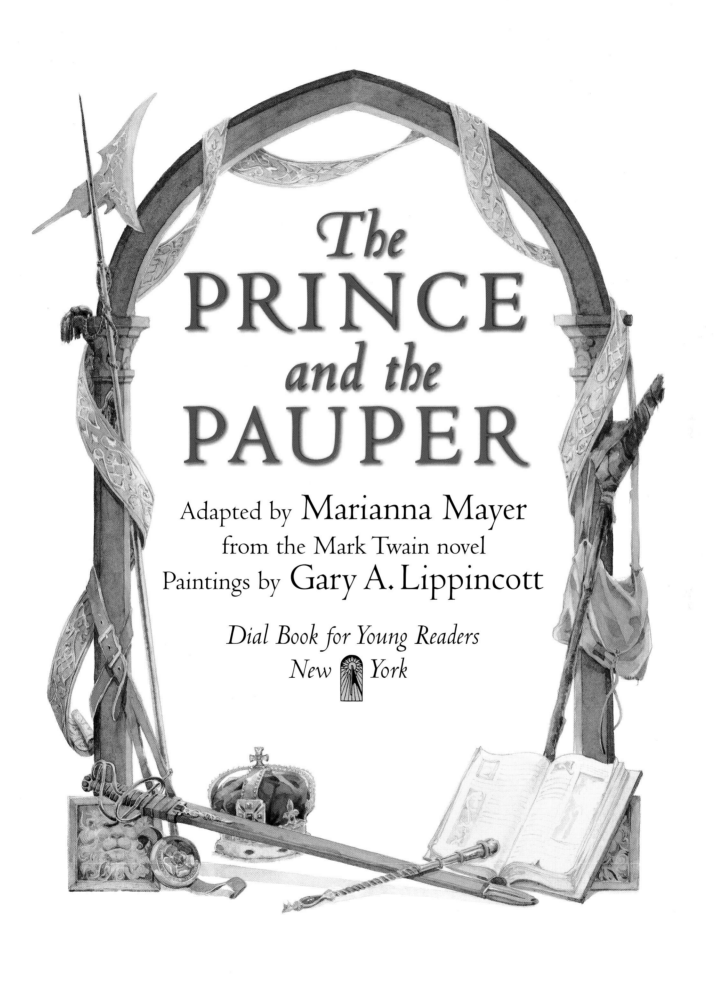

The PRINCE and the PAUPER

Adapted by Marianna Mayer
from the Mark Twain novel
Paintings by Gary A. Lippincott

Dial Book for Young Readers
New York

For Larry Grigely—a true and princely friend
M. M.

To my family
G. A. L.

Published by Dial Books for Young Readers
A division of Penguin Putnam Inc.
345 Hudson Street
New York, New York 10014

Text copyright © 1999 by Marianna Mayer
Paintings copyright © 1999 by Gary A. Lippincott
Designed by Atha Tehon
Printed in Hong Kong on acid-free paper
First Edition
1 3 5 7 9 10 8 6 4 2

Library of Congress Cataloging in Publication Data
Mayer, Marianna.
The prince and the pauper/adapted by Marianna Mayer;
paintings by Gary A. Lippincott.—1st ed.
p.   cm.
Summary: A simplified retelling of the Mark Twain classic in which
young Edward VI of England and a poor boy who resembles him exchange places
and each learns something about the other's very different station in life.
ISBN 0-8037-2099-8
1. Edward VI, King of England, 1537-1553—Juvenile fiction.
[1. Edward VI, King of England, 1537-1553—Fiction. 2. Mistaken identity—Fiction.
3. Adventure and adventurers—Fiction. 4. England—Fiction.]
I. Twain, Mark, 1835-1910. Prince and the pauper. II. Lippincott, Gary A., ill. III. Title.
PZ7.M4617Pr 1999
[Fic]—dc21   98-36176   CIP   AC

The paintings for this book were created with watercolors.

Samuel Langhorne Clemens (1835-1910), also known as Mark Twain, the renowned novelist, humorist, and satirist, remains one of the greatest writers America has ever produced. Famed for *The Adventures of Tom Sawyer* (1876), and *The Adventures of Huckleberry Finn* (1884), Mark Twain authored a number of novels, including *The Prince and the Pauper*. Written in 1882, *The Prince and the Pauper* was first undertaken as an entertainment for two of Twain's daughters, Susy and Clara. Dedicated to them both, the novel was regarded by his daughters as their father's best work; their mother, Livy, agreed.

Set in sixteenth-century England, the story's basic premise is the exchange of roles between the young prince and the pauper. Twain liked using the theme of switching identities, and returned to it often in his writings. And as was the case in both "Tom Sawyer" and "Huck Finn," the heart of the plot for *The Prince and the Pauper* relies on the experiences of two young boys. Their exchange of roles results in a loss of innocence and gradual gain of an understanding of the world.

An avid reader of history, Twain yoked together the ingredients of myth and legend with historical fact to create his stories. Though *The Prince and the Pauper* is certainly fiction, Twain borrowed from history to bolster the plot. The real-life character of Edward VI, born October 12, 1537 in London's Hampton Court, is cast opposite the imagined Tom Canty. Edward was the only child of Henry VIII by his third wife, Jane Seymour. His mother died only twelve days after his birth, and Edward himself was a frail child who was never expected to live a long life. This did not prevent a strenuous education; he was fluent in Latin, Greek, and French. On January 28, 1547, amidst a period of political and religious repression enforced by harsh laws, Edward, then only nine years of age, succeeded his father as king. His health began to fail in 1552, and on July 6, 1553, he died before reaching his sixteenth birthday.

Twain believed the young king's brief reign to be singularly merciful for that cruel era. Yet there is hardly a trace of Edward's personal influence on the course of history, since his kingship seems to have been controlled by his chief advisor, the Earl of Warwick. Nevertheless, Edward VI is remembered for having manifested exceptional and precocious talent, evidenced by his writings, which reflect an acute awareness of the evils of the time.

The greatest difficulty for any writer when attempting to adapt a novel to the picture book form comes when deciding what to leave in and what to omit. At best it is an agonizing struggle, for the goal surely is to tell a good story regardless of the length, and at the same time to remain faithful to the original intent of the source.

Though in no way a substitute for Mark Twain's *The Prince and the Pauper*, this edition is intended to create a delight in reading for the young child, as well as an introduction and inspiration for future readings of Twain's works as the reader matures.

Marianna Mayer, Riverview Farm

ONCE THERE WAS A PRINCE who became a ragged pauper and a ragged pauper who became a prince. It all began long ago when a boy named Tom was born to the wretchedly poor Canty family, who did not want him. On the same day another boy named Edward was born to the royal Tudor family, who wanted him very much. Indeed the whole country celebrated, for he was Edward, Prince of Wales, and would one day be king of all England.

As the years passed, the two boys began to look so much alike that their own mothers could not have told them apart. Yet their lives were very different.

Prince Edward acquired knowledge of the world through his tutors, while Tom grew to know the world by begging along the London streets. But Tom had a tutor as well, Father Andrew, a kindly old priest. He saw that Tom was bright, and so encouraged him to learn Latin, history, reading, and writing. Most of all Tom loved the stories the priest told about King Arthur and his noble knights. To escape his dreary life, Tom daydreamed, casting himself as a prince who fought dragons and rescued princesses. At night he would lie awake wishing, If only I could see a real prince just once.

One day in January while Tom was out begging, he wandered very far from home and found himself before a grand palace. When he spied a young boy crossing the royal courtyard, he thought, His clothes are so fine, he *must* be a prince.

The next instant Tom was thrown to the ground. "Get away from here, you filthy beggar," said a palace guard, about to strike Tom again.

"Stop!" commanded Prince Edward, for indeed that was whom Tom had seen. "How dare you treat the lad in such a manner. Bring him to me at once!

"You look cold and hungry," the prince said to Tom. "Come with me."

"Are you sure?" stammered Tom.

"Certainly, don't be afraid. I am Prince Edward."

The boys went to Edward's chambers, and Tom was allowed to look at everything and to ask as many questions as he wished. Edward, too, had all sorts of questions. "Do you really swim in the river? And play in mud holes? Oh, I would give up my crown to dress as you and revel in the mud just once."

Tom smiled humbly. "And if I could wear your finery just once, sweet sir—"

"So be it!" said the prince. "Let me try on your clothes and you may try on mine." The exchange was made, and as the prince and the pauper stared at each other, Edward said, "Why, look in the mirror, we could be twins!"

Then he saw the nasty bruise on Tom's hand. "Did the guard do this?"

"Yes, Your Highness, but it's nothing," said Tom.

"*Nothing!*" declared the prince. "I shall have him punished. Wait here." And with that, Edward stormed off.

When he reached the gate, he called, "Open up!" The guard obeyed, but as the prince stepped out, the guard struck him down. "That's for getting me in trouble with the prince."

"I *am* the Prince of Wales! You'll be hanged for this outrage!" shouted Edward, but he was wearing Tom's rags.

"Get out of here or you'll get worse from me," threatened the guard, and he threw Edward out onto the muddy street.

"Let me back in!" ordered Edward amidst hoots from the gathering crowd.

"He is quite mad," they said. Some even threw stones at him as they hustled him far down the road. Edward began to run, though he had no idea where he was going. By nightfall, lost and confused, he stumbled upon the very neighborhood where Tom had said he lived.

Suddenly a large brute of a man grabbed him. "Where have you been, you little wretch? I'll beat you for being late or my name is not John Canty!"

"Canty!" shouted Edward. "Are you really Tom's father?"

"*His* father? I am *your* father!"

"Oh, please, sir," Edward begged. "You must come with me and convince the palace guards that I am the Prince of Wales."

"Prince of *what*?!" scoffed Canty. "You've gone off your head is what. A good beating will straighten you out."

"Let me go!" cried the boy.

Just then Father Andrew came upon them in the dark. When he saw Canty beating the boy, he shouted, "Stop! Leave him be!"

In a flash Canty turned on the priest and knocked him down. "I'll do the same to you if you don't get upstairs *now*," he told Edward.

Canty's wife, daughters, and his wretched old mother were waiting in the flat. "Here is your good-for-nothing son," he shouted at his wife. "Now he's gone insane. Listen." Turning to Edward he said, "So tell us who you are."

"I've told you, I'm Edward, Prince of Wales," said the boy.

Tom's mother began to wail. "Oh, poor Tom, it's all those books you read that's done this to you."

"Please, madam," said Edward, "your son is fine. Take me to the palace, and the king will see he is returned to you."

"I've had enough of this nonsense," said Canty. "Off to bed, all of you!"

Resigned for the moment, the exhausted prince fell on a bundle of rags and went to sleep. But Mrs. Canty lay awake with the nagging sense that perhaps the boy was not her son. She finally decided to make a test. "Tom always puts his hand before his eyes when he is startled," she recalled. "I'll wake him, and if he does it, I'll be satisfied." But though she made the test several times during the night, the boy never moved his hand.

Near dawn one of Canty's friends came with news. "John, someone saw you strike Father Andrew and now he is dying. You had better run or be hanged for murder."

"Quick!" Canty shouted to his family. "We're moving on." They fled the flat, and for safety's sake they separated. But Canty told Edward, "You're staying with me."

In the street, Canty let go of the boy just long enough for the prince to break away; the next instant he was off and running.

"Why isn't anyone from the palace out looking for me?" Edward wondered. "Don't they know I'm missing? Tom must be having fun passing himself off as me. I'll have him hanged for it!"

But Tom was not having fun. After Edward had left him, he waited a long time, becoming more frightened by the moment. Then a door opened. "Who is it?" he called anxiously.

Much to his regret, it was not the prince, but a young lady. "Why, my lord, it is only me, Lady Grey. What is wrong?"

Tom fell to his knees. "Have mercy. I'm not the prince, but Tom Canty. Please tell the prince to return my clothes and let me go home."

"My lord, you must be ill," said Lady Grey. "I will tell the king at once."

She soon returned, bringing with her a group of nobles. Again Tom tried to explain who he was, but to no avail. "Indeed, Sire, you *are* ill," said one. "Please come with us." Tom continued to protest as they ushered him into a chamber where King Henry VIII lay bedridden from a long illness.

"Here now, Edward, what is all this about?" the king asked.

"Please, Sire, I am not the prince."

The king shook his head. "I will make a test." Then he asked the boy a question in Latin. Father Andrew had schooled Tom well, and he answered correctly. "Good," said the king. "All is not lost. He will recover. Meanwhile the doctors say I do not have much time left. I want my son pronounced heir to the throne tonight."

When Lord Hertford, the king's Lord Chancellor, heard the news, he went to the king. "Sire, have you the Great Seal? We cannot carry out the order without it."

"The Great Seal is with my son," said the king. "Ask him for it. But do not distress him."

Lord Hertford explained the situation to Tom, who of course had no idea what the Great Seal was. Rather than upset him any further it was decided that the Small Seal would have to be used.

Tom was still fretting over his predicament when Lord Hertford returned to escort him to dinner. "I'm *not* the prince," Tom tried to explain.

But Lord Hertford said gently, "Please, Sire, you must not keep saying that."

"I suppose it does no good," said Tom.

And so he allowed himself to be pressed into the princely duties expected of Edward. Alas he made many mistakes. At dinner, he ate with his hands, refusing to wipe them on his linen napkin. "It is too pretty," he said. "I will soil it." And when he was served a finger bowl filled with rose water to wash his hands, he drank it and said, "This is a very flavorless soup." At the end of the meal, he greedily filled his pockets with nuts from the table. "In case I get hungry later," he explained to everyone's amazement.

But unlike the cruel treatment Edward was receiving for his supposed madness, Tom was given every consideration. Cleverly, he used his apparent loss of memory to find out the things he needed to know.

After staying up long past midnight reading etiquette books, Tom awoke the next day not knowing where he was and called for his mother. In her place came a bevy of servants. To Tom's surprise, they addressed him as *king!* King Henry, they explained, had died during the night.

With much fanfare, the servants selected what Tom should wear. He was washed and dressed, then taken into the throne room with great ceremony. The splendors of the assembly delighted Tom's eyes and fired his imagination, at first. Yet the speeches were long and dreary, so what began as a pleasure grew into weariness.

Later Tom presided at the Hall of Justice to hear the cases of the condemned. A man, a woman, and a small child were led in by soldiers. The man, explained the sheriff in charge, was to be executed for taking another's life by poison. Tom looked at the prisoner and a vague memory stirred him. Indeed he recalled seeing this very man on New Year's Day save a drowning boy.

"Majesty, I am innocent," said the man, "but I beg you, let me be hanged."

"You beg to be *hanged?*" Tom asked.

"Yes, Majesty, for I am to be boiled alive."

"What kind of justice is this!" exclaimed Tom. "Let no more poor creatures be given such torture."

Lord Hertford smiled. "The practice shall be abolished immediately, Your Grace, and history will remember you for it."

A buzz of admiration swept through the assemblage. "This is no mad king," some remarked. "He has his wits about him surely."

Tom turned to the sheriff. "Name the day and place where the deed was done."

"New Year's Day, Sire, in the hamlet of Islington."

Tom knew firsthand that the prisoner could not have committed the crime, for Islington was many miles from London. "Let the prisoner go free. It is the king's will."

Now he was eager to know what deadly doings the woman and child had done.

"Through their wicked power," the sheriff explained, "they invoked a storm that wasted an entire village."

"How was the storm brought on exactly?" Tom asked.

"By pulling off their stockings, Sire."

Amazed, Tom turned to the woman. "Use your power now, for I wish to see such a storm." Seeing the puzzled look on the woman's face, he added, "Never fear—exert your power, and you and the child shall go free."

The woman cried, "Oh, my lord, I cannot."

"I promise you full pardon for such a wonder," said Tom. The woman threw herself down and swore she had no such power.

Finally Tom said, "I think she speaks truly. Be at ease, good woman. You and the child may go. But first, pull off your stockings."

The woman obeyed, stripping her own feet and the child's, but it did not produce so much as a drop of rain.

"There good soul," Tom said, "your power has departed. Go in peace."

At the close of the session Tom declared, "From this day forward the king's law shall be a law of mercy, not a law of blood."

Edward was not managing as well. Having escaped Canty, he returned to the palace to try to gain entry. A crowd gathered around him. Some people laughed and began to curse him, while others prodded him with sticks. Then a tall man came forward. "Leave the poor lad alone," he said, raising his sword.

"Who is this?" mocked one bully. "Another prince in disguise, no doubt."

"My name is Miles Hendon," said the man. "Harm this boy and you'll answer to me."

Just then royal troops came thundering past the gates. "Make way," they called. "The king is dead!"

At the news bedlam broke out. Miles Hendon took hold of Edward, and they began to race through the streets with crowds shouting all around them. "King Henry is dead! Long live the new king!"

Edward stopped to listen and tears filled his eyes. "My father is dead?"

"Your father?" said Miles. "Of course, I almost forgot. You are Edward, Prince of Wales, and now King Edward." But Miles was thinking, Poor lad, he is quite out of his head. Perhaps if I humor him, he will improve. Whatever happens, I am bound to look after him, for clearly he hasn't a friend in the world.

Miles brought the boy to an inn. "It is a humble place, my prince. You see, I have just returned from the war after seven years. When we get to my home at Hendon Hall, I shall look after you properly."

As they entered the inn, neither saw John Canty lurking in the shadows across the street.

Miles gave the boy his doublet, for the room was chilly. Then he called for the innkeeper to bring their supper. When the meal arrived, Edward sat down, but as Miles moved to sit, Edward frowned. "You cannot sit in the presence of the king."

"Yes, yes, Your Highness. But if you would grant me the privilege, it would certainly make our lives a bit easier."

"It is a most unusual request," said Edward thoughtfully. "But your point is well taken. I shall grant your wish."

"Thank you, Sire," said Miles as he sat down with a great sigh.

After supper Edward climbed into the only bed.

"And where, Sire, am I to sleep?" asked Miles.

"I dub you knight, Sir Miles, the king's protector. You must sleep beside the door and guard it."

Miles smiled and shook his head. "So I am now a knight of the Kingdom of Dreams and Shadows." He stretched out across the threshold thinking what a king the little lad would make. One might even suppose it was in his blood.

Early next morning while Edward was sound asleep, Miles set out to buy the boy a proper suit of clothes. But when he returned an hour later, the lad was gone.

"He went off with your messenger," explained the innkeeper, "right after you left."

"I sent no messenger!" said Miles as he stormed out onto the streets.

But Edward was long gone. In truth it was Canty who'd sent the messenger, a young ruffian named Hugo. "Is it much further?" Edward asked him.

"Just a bit," said Hugo.

At last they came to an abandoned barn, and to Edward's horror he discovered that not Miles but John Canty was waiting. With him was a host of thieves and beggars.

"I've got you now!" said Canty, roughly grabbing Edward.

The leader of the gang went over to the boy. "And who might this be?"

"I'm King Edward," said the boy before Canty could answer.

"Really? Well, King, here are your subjects. Speak up, lads. Here's your chance to speak directly to your king."

A man named Jack stood up. "I've a brief tale and 'tis quickly told. I and most of my comrades were left wandering and hungry because our farms were taken over to make way for sheep ranges. Without jobs, we were forced to beg and were whipped for it. But we had no other means to survive except to go begging again. Those who were caught were whipped again, and deprived of an ear, but went begging a third time—what else could they do—and were branded with a red-hot iron, then sold as slaves. Some ran, were hunted down, and hanged. Others of us fared less badly. Stand up, Yokel, Burn, and Hodge—show your trophies."

These stood and stripped away their shirts, exposing old welts left by the lash. One turned up his hair and showed where a left ear had once been. Another revealed a shoulder branded with the letter *V* for "vagrant." The third told how his wife and baby had died of starvation. "They are better off," he said sadly, "for being out of this world."

"What do you say to that, King?" asked the leader, smirking.

"I am deeply touched," Edward answered. "You shall not suffer so in the future—this day marks the end of such cruelty."

"Very good, Sire, and we shall crown you Foo Foo the First, the Mooncalf King." Then hoisting him up, they sat Edward on a barrel, and crowned him with an old tin pot.

Shortly after, Canty grabbed Edward. "I'm sick of your delusions. Tomorrow you and Hugo are going out to do some stealing."

That night Canty's eyes never left the boy while Edward pretended to sleep. In the wee hours Canty began to snore. Edward acted in a moment. He ran as fast as he could into the forest with only moonlight to guide him.

Finally he stopped to catch his breath. The moon cast an eerie light on the trees, and shadows loomed all around him. Suddenly he heard a twig snap. Edward held his breath, too frightened to move. Just then a voice called out, "Is that you, my prince?" It was Miles Hendon, who had been trailing Edward since morning. Never was a man more welcome, and Edward threw his arms around his friend in relief.

At first light they set out for Hendon Hall. "Once we get there," said Miles, "I will see that you are looked after properly. You'll have a chance to rest."

"That I shall welcome, indeed," said the young king.

"And you'll meet my father and my youngest brother, Alfred," Miles continued. "He is a fine lad. And Hugh, my other brother—we've never gotten on. But bless me, I believe I will even be happy to see him again."

When they at last reached Hendon Hall, Miles took Edward's hand and eagerly rushed inside. They found Sir Hugh Hendon seated at a writing table in a grand room. As Miles went to embrace him, Hugh rose and demanded, "What is the meaning of this? Who are you?"

"Why, I'm your brother Miles! Seven years hasn't changed me that much."

"My brother died in battle three years ago. I have the letter to prove it. You are an impostor."

"That's a lie! Call Father and Alfred. They'll know me."

"My father and younger brother are dead as well," replied Sir Hugh.

"Dead! Mercy on their kind souls, what terrible news!" Tears came to Miles' eyes.

"Enough!" said Hugh. "Now get out or I'll have you arrested."

Miles caught him by the throat. "What is this? You know me! You'll admit the truth if I have to wring it out of you!"

Servants came rushing into the room and dragged Miles away.

"Don't let this criminal escape!" cried Hugh.

"I have no intention of leaving," said Miles, pulling himself free.

Hugh staggered to his feet and went to summon the authorities. Edward sat down quietly next to Miles, who was deep in thought. Finally the door opened and soldiers took them away.

"In you go," snarled the prison guard as he threw Miles and Edward into a dimly lighted cell. There among the many prisoners, they saw two women—a mother and her daughter.

"Poor lad," they said to Edward. "Don't be afraid." That night when the prisoners were given their meal, the women saved the best bits of theirs for Edward. And under their gentle care, he found some peace.

"Why are you in prison?" he asked them the next day. They said it was because they were Baptists.

"What crime is that?" he said. "Surely you'll be released in no time, and I shall lose two dear friends."

Later all the prisoners were led into the jail yard. Horrified, Edward saw both mother and daughter tied to a stake. Wood was piled at their feet and then set aflame.

With tear-filled eyes Edward vowed, "I shall never forget this day if I live to be one hundred."

After the prisoners were returned to their cells, Edward overheard the guards saying that the new king would be crowned in two days. "Miles, did you hear? They're crowning someone else in my place. We've got to get to Westminster and stop them!"

"Calm yourself, Sire," Miles said. "My trial is tomorrow. We will get there in time."

The next day Miles and Edward were brought before the judge.

Miles' rightful claim to the Hendon estate was ignored. Instead he was sentenced to two hours in the pillory for attacking Sir Hugh. "The boy can go free," said the judge, "though he must give up the company of riffraff like you."

"How dare you!" shouted Edward. "Set him free. I command it."

The judge called the guards. "Give this fool boy a good lashing—it will teach him to hold his tongue."

"Please, Your Honor," Miles interrupted. "See how young and frail he is. I will take the lashing in his place." And so it was that Miles received the whipping meant for Edward.

Afterward the king came softly to Miles' side and whispered, "This noble deed shall never be wiped from my memory. You saved the king not only from pain, but humiliation." He picked up the whip from the ground, touched Hendon's bleeding shoulder lightly with it, and said, "Edward, King of England, dubs you earl."

Miles was touched, his eyes filled, yet he was struck by the grisly humor of the situation—the specter-knight of the Kingdom of Dreams and Shadows now an earl!

Hendon was released on the day of the coronation, and Edward was waiting. "Is there time?" asked the boy. "Will we reach Westminster in time?"

"Don't fret, Sire," Miles answered, "we'll be there in plenty of time." In truth, Miles had his own reasons to return to London. For if he could find a certain nobleman who was once his father's friend, the man might help Miles with his claim to Hendon Hall.

Together Miles and Edward hurried to London, and as they entered the city, they found a glorious celebration under way.

Meanwhile Tom was just waking up. Servants fluttered about to prepare him for the coronation ceremony. I'm getting to like this life, thought Tom.

He rode on a prancing war steed to the coronation, and Lord Hertford gave him a bag of coins to distribute among the crowds. Suddenly a particular woman caught his eye. Up flew his hand to his face in that old, involuntary gesture. It was his mother.

"Tom!" she called out. "My darling boy, it's you, isn't it?"

Her face full of love, she rushed toward Tom. But the guards held her back. Tom watched in silence as the procession moved on.

His attendants saw how dejected he became, and tried to encourage him to wave to the people. Tom only shook his head and whispered quietly, "She was my mother."

A glittering stream of nobility flowed into the great hall. When Tom Canty entered with his entourage, all rose. Triumphant music burst forth, and Tom, clothed in regal robes, was conducted to the throne. As the Archbishop of Canterbury held the crown over the trembling boy's head, there came a sudden shout.

"I forbid you to set the crown upon this impostor's head! *I* am the king."
Everyone turned to see a shabbily dressed boy emerge from his hiding place. The
guards apprehended him immediately.

But Tom stood up and declared, "I command you to turn him loose. He *is* the
true king!"

At these words, panic broke out. "Pay His Majesty no mind," instructed Lord
Hertford. "His illness is upon him once more. Seize the vagabond!"

Tom called again more loudly, "He *is* the true king!" He ran to Edward and knelt
before him. Only then did the others notice the uncanny resemblance between the
two boys.

Lord Hertford had an idea. "If you are the true king, then where is the Great Seal?"

Edward smiled. "A simple question." Then he told them where to look. A messenger went to find it, only to return declaring it was not there.

"How could you have missed such a huge golden disk?" asked Edward in disbelief.

"Take him away!" shouted Lord Hertford.

"Wait!" Tom called out. "Sire, was it not on the table when we first went into your chamber?" Edward nodded. "Well then, do you recall the last thing you did before you left the room?"

Edward's face brightened. "Of course! I looked for a place to put the Great Seal." Turning to the messenger, he said, "Go back! Look in the suit of armor in my chamber."

The messenger left and quickly brought back the seal, and the entire assemblage fell to its knees before the king.

"How on earth did you know where the Great Seal was?" Edward asked Tom.

"I didn't until you described it, for in truth I've been using it all this time as a nutcracker."

Edward was restored to his throne, and that very day he called an assembly. When Miles Hendon came forward, the young monarch said, "Know you all ladies, lords, and gentlemen, that this man, Miles Hendon, is my trusty and well-loved servant. He is a peer of England, Earl of Kent, and shall have gold and lands to equal none."

Then Sir Hugh Hendon and young Tom Canty were brought forward. Turning to Sir Hugh, the king commanded, "Have this robber stripped of his stolen estate, and put under lock and key." To Tom, who was most handsomely dressed, he said, "I have learned the story of your efforts and am well pleased, Tom. You have governed the realm with royal gentleness and mercy.

"You, your mother and sisters shall live under the king's protection all the rest of your days, and you shall bear the title of the King's Ward. As for your father, he shall be found and hanged, if you so desire. Henceforth you shall wear the special robe of state, for once you were a king, and none shall fail to give you reverence."

Indeed Tom Canty, who lived to be a very old and distinguished man, was honored all the days of his life. Wherever he went, the crowd parted to make way for him, and whispered, "Take off your hat, for it is good King Edward's Ward!" In return they would get Tom's ever warm and kindly smile.

As for Edward, he lived far too briefly, but worthily. He was never to forget those unfortunates he'd met during the time he lived in poverty as a despised pauper. He kept the promises he'd made to all of them, but more than that, the promises he'd made to himself to always rule with gentleness and mercy.